RUPERT
and the
WOBBLY
WITCH

CARNIVAL

Rupert is going to a party tonight, and Mrs Bear is making him a special costume to wear.

It is a Hallowe'en party – so you can guess what Rupert will be dressed as.

You're right – he is going as a GHOST!

While Mrs Bear is busy sewing up the costume, Rupert wanders off to play.

As he nears the woods, a sudden crash makes the birds flutter off their branches in alarm. Something has fallen into the brambles.

A strange figure in black crawls out and flops down in front of Rupert!

Rupert catches sight of a mop of
golden curls under the stranger's
hat.

'Why, you're a girl,' he exclaims.

She looks up at him shakily. 'My broomstick,' she mutters. 'What happened to my broomstick?'

She limps back to the bushes and returns a moment or two later in tears.

'It's broken,' she sobs. 'The handle's come off and it's all smashed up. Whatever shall I do?'

'Don't worry,' says Rupert kindly. 'I'm sure we have a brush or a rake at home you can use.'

'You don't understand.' She shakes her head in despair. 'It's not for sweeping. It's for FLYING.'

Rupert stares at her in amazement. 'But – but –,' he stammers, 'that's what WITCHES do!'

'But I AM a witch,' she cries
miserably.

The tears stream down her face.

'I know I don't look like a witch, and my hair's the wrong colour, but I am, I really am. The other witches won't let me go out with them because I can't fly my broomstick very well and I keep falling off. And tonight is Hallowe'en and it's NOT FAIR!'

Rupert sits down weakly, not sure he can believe his ears!

'Perhaps it can be mended,' he suggests, finding his voice at last. He searches among the bushes and gathers up the broken parts of the broomstick.

Then with some string and a penknife he binds the broken handle together and ties it back on as firmly as he can.

'See if that works,' he tells her.

She sets off gingerly and flies
slowly round the bushes and
back.

'It's a bit wobbly,' she gasps, 'but I'm sure it will get me home.'

Rupert has another idea. 'There's a Hallowe'en party in Bill Badger's garden tonight,' he says excitedly. 'You can go there and practice!'

'A Hallowe'en party!' She claps her hands in delight. 'Oh, what fun!'

Then her face clouds over. 'But I don't LOOK much like a witch, do I? I'm not ugly enough and my hair's all wrong.'

Rupert thinks for a moment.
'Wait here,' he says.

He races home and returns with
his finger paints, a mirror and an
old floormop!

He splodges white paint on her
face, puts black lines round her
eyes, and then dabs a horrid
green colour on her cheeks and
neck.

After that, he fixes the floormop
on her head to cover up her curls!

She sees herself in the mirror and
squeals with glee. 'I look like a
proper witch now,' she beams.

Rupert points out the cottage
where Bill lives. 'Arrive at about
six o'clock,' he tells her. 'It will be

dark by then and everyone will be
in the garden.'

Sure enough, that evening when the party is in full swing, the little witch swoops in over the tree-tops on her broken broomstick, cackling and shaking her fist!

Rupert pretends to be as astonished as everyone else!

'I hope she doesn't fall off,' he thinks to himself.

He breathes a sigh of relief when, with a final screech, she flits away in the moonlight without crashing!

'Crumbs, did you see THAT?' gulps Bill. 'Fancy a REAL witch coming to my party. What a treat!'

But Mrs Badger gives Rupert a strange look. 'I saw that horrid old witch WINK at you, Rupert,' she says.

And, of course, that's exactly what she HAD done – but Rupert is determined not to tell anyone why!

Or to let anyone know that she isn't horrid or old at all!

He dashes off to join in the apple-bobbing before Mrs. Badger can utter another word!

Will you promise to keep the little witch's secret, too?

Carnival
An imprint of the Children's Division
of the Collins Publishing Group
8 Grafton Street, London W1X 3LA

First published by Dragon Books 1986
Published by Carnival 1988

Written by Len Collis
Illustrated by Jon Davis
Designed by Ralph Semmence
Copyright © The Nutwood Press Ltd 1986
Copyright © Title and character of Rupert Bear,
Express Newspapers plc 1986

ISBN 0 00 1944 56 8

Printed & bound in Great Britain by
PURNELL BOOK PRODUCTION LIMITED
A MEMBER OF BPCC plc